leapfrog
World
Tales

Chief
Five Heads

A Southern African tale
told by Margaret Nash

Illustrated by Anni Axworthy

FRANKLIN WATTS
LONDON • SYDNEY

First published in 2009 by
Franklin Watts
338 Euston Road
London
NW1 3BH

Franklin Watts Australia
Level 17/207 Kent Street
Sydney
NSW 2000

A CIP catalogue record for this book is available
from the British Library.

ISBN 978 0 7496 8593 5 (hbk)
ISBN 978 0 7496 8599 7 (pbk)

Series Editor: Jackie Hamley
Series Advisor: Dr Barrie Wade
Series Designer: Peter Scoulding

Printed in China

Franklin Watts is a division of
Hachette Children's Books,
an Hachette UK company
www.hachette.co.uk

This tale comes from Southern Africa. Can you find this area on a map?

Once upon a time, a father told his daughters of a chief who wanted a wife.

"I should be the wife of a chief!" said the elder daughter. And she left.

Soon she met a mouse. "Shall I show you the way?" he asked.

"Go away! I am too important to talk to a mouse!" the girl shouted.

Then she met an old
woman who started
to say something.

The girl would not listen
to her and walked away
as fast as she could.

Next she met a hungry
goat-boy. "May I have
some food?" he asked.

"NO!" she snapped at him, finishing her lunch.

At the village, the chief's sister told her, "Don't be scared of my brother."

12

"I'm not scared of anything!" laughed the girl rudely.

That night, the wind
howled. The chief blew in!

He was an ugly snake
with five heads. The girl
ran away screaming.

The elder daughter
trudged home.

"Now I will go," said the younger daughter.

Soon she met a mouse.
"Shall I show you the
way?" he asked.

"Yes, please," said the girl.

Next she met an old woman. "Take the little path," she said.

"Thank you," said the girl.

Then she met a hungry goat-boy. "May I have some food?" he asked. "Of course," said the girl.

"Be kind to the woman by the stream," he told her. "I shall," said the girl.

By the stream, the girl
met the chief's sister.
"Don't be scared of my
brother," she said.

"I shall not be scared.
Thank you," said the girl.

That night, the wind howled. In blew the chief. The girl smiled bravely.

"I saw how kind you were," he said, "for I was the mouse, the old woman and the goat-boy."

27

Then Chief Five Heads became a handsome young man.

And he and the younger
daughter lived happily
ever after.

Puzzle 1

Put these pictures in the correct order.
Now tell the story in your own words.
What different endings can you think of?

Puzzle 2

gentle   polite
bad-tempered

nasty   generous
mean

wise   careful
silly

Choose the correct adjectives for each character. Which adjectives are incorrect? Turn over to find the answers.

Answers

Puzzle 1

The correct order is: 1c, 2f, 3a, 4b, 5d, 6e

Puzzle 2

Elder daughter: the correct adjective is bad-tempered

The incorrect adjectives are gentle, polite

Younger daughter: the correct adjective is generous

The incorrect adjectives are mean, nasty

The chief: the correct adjectives are careful, wise

The incorrect adjective is silly

Look out for Leapfrog fairy tales:

For more Leapfrog books go to: www.franklinwatts.co.uk